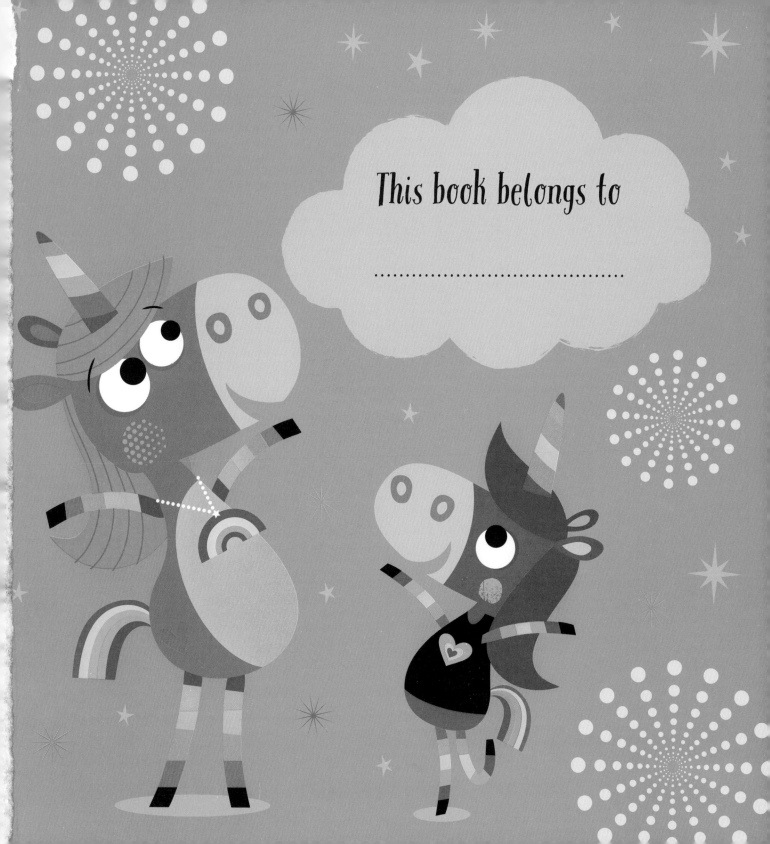

This book belongs to

....

My ENCHANTED
Storytime Treasury

make
believe
ideas

CONTENTS

We are the grOovicOrns!

ROSIE GREENING ★ STUART LYNCH

Everyone **loves** unicorns. They always make a fuss.
But you know who **should** be famous?

I ♥ unicorns!

The grOOViCOrns!

That's us!

The unicorns make **rainbows**

that **curve** from side to side.

our rainbows **never** look right,

Good work,
Topsy!

Groovicorn
Inspector

12

but they make
amazing slides!

Unicorns sign hoofprints,

My Unicorn Scrapbook

To Rabbit,

Love Glitter

14

Show-off.

and they grant your **WiSHeS**, too.

HAPPY BIRTHDAY

We don't have
magic powers,

but we still make **dreams** come true!

Buckinghorn Palace

18

The unicorns build
Palaces

with sweet
marshmallow walls.

No adoring fans allowed

EEW, unicorn palaces are **GROSS!**

19

We have **multicolored** tents

All WELcOME

The unicorns
**bring
sunshine**
everywhere
they go.

23

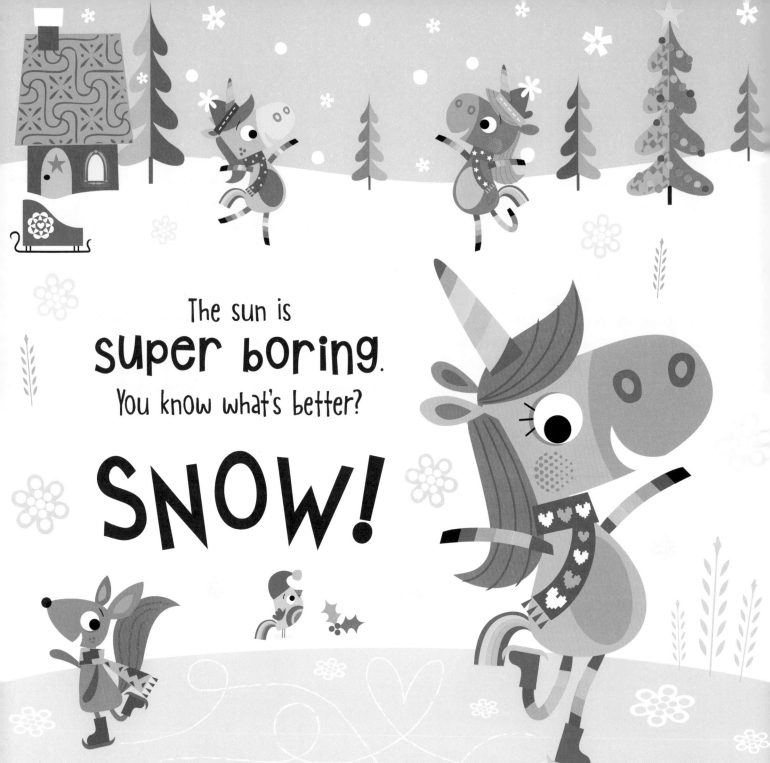

The sun is **super boring.** You know what's better?

SNOW!

24

25

It's **hard** to be a **unicorn** –
we have a **lot** to do.

There's **never**
any time to play.
We wish we were
like **YOU!**

To Do
Make rainbow
*
Grant wish
*
Rainbow school
*
Hoofprint signing
*
Mane maintenance
*
Polish hooves
*
Attend premiere

29

and this is how you **Sliiiiiiiiide**.

Nice rainbow, Ronald!

EVERYthing
is much more fun
if we **PLAY** side by side!

31

Everyone is different, but special in their way.

So let's learn from one another and have more fun every day!

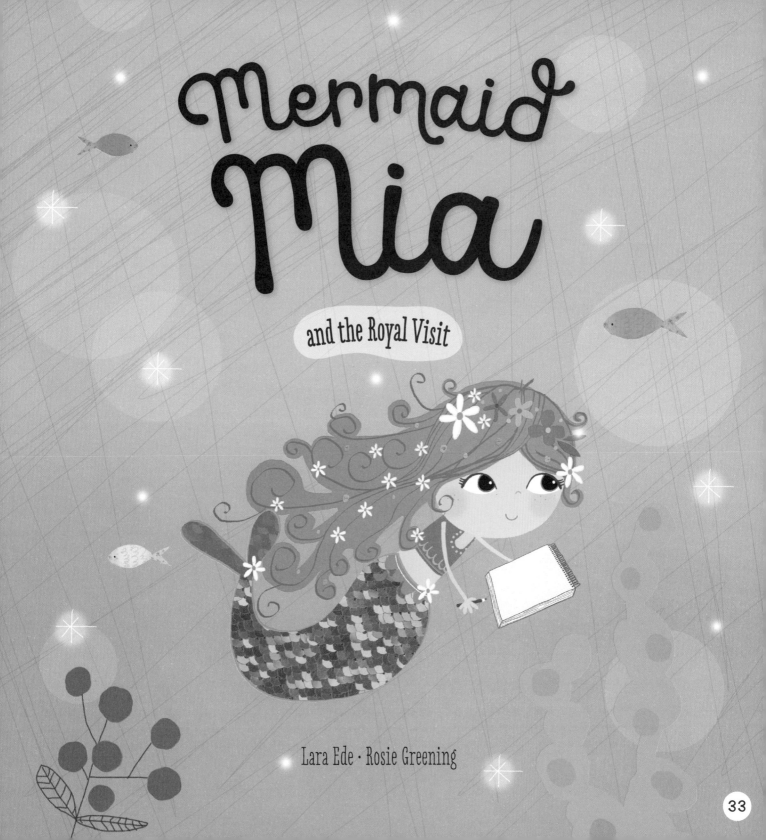

Mermaid Mia

and the Royal Visit

Lara Ede · Rosie Greening

Mermaid Mia loved to write
new **stories** every day.

Ideas

34

She ran the **paper** at her school with **Emily** and **Fay**.

Emily took the **photographs** ...

Say cheese!

and Fay did the **reviews.**

The Mermail

But **Mia** was the one in charge of each day's **front-page** news.

Mia's news was **popular** and **always** told with style.

Wow! What a story!

Ha-ha!

The Mermail

She was funny, frank, and honest, and her **words** made people smile.

One morning, **Mia** longed to find a juicy piece of **news.**

She got her **pad** and went in **search** of **something** she could use.

Her first lead was a story
on the **snails** in the canteen.

But the **news** was **so** s-l-o-w – m-o-v-i-n-g, Mia **really** wasn't keen.

Then she heard a **rumor** of a **whale** stuck in the **gym**.

"Now **that's** a story," **Mia** thought. "I'll write my news on him!"

1, 2, 3, push!

STARFISH ACAD

But just as **Mia** reached the **whale**, he managed to get **out**.

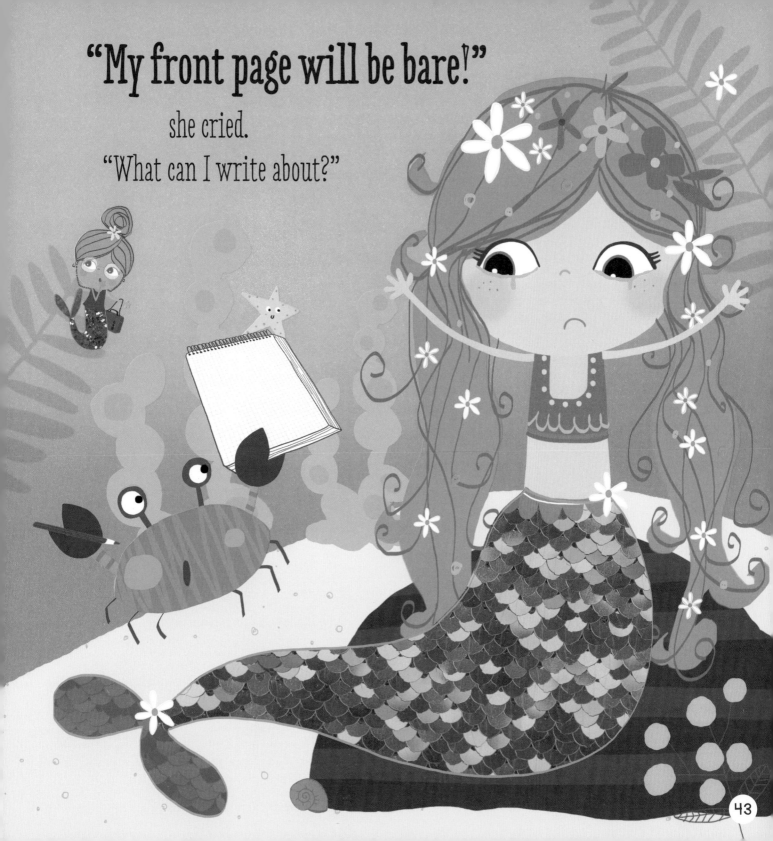

"My front page will be bare!"
she cried.
"What can I write about?"

43

Suddenly, a sneaky thought **popped** into **Mia's** head.

"The **real** news isn't good enough –
I'll **make it up** instead!"

She **swam** back to the newsroom
and began to type full speed.

"This **news** will make a **splash**," she thought.
"They're **sure** to want to read!"

The Mermail

Queen Marina is one of the most popular royals under the sea. Whether it's recycling in the coral beds, or opening libraries, the queen always has a new project on the go. Just last month, it was Queen Marina's birthday. It was a magical day, with tasty treats, a fantastic band, and comedy from the clown fish.

The biggest gift Queen Marina received was a beautiful carriage, though it has yet to be used out in public. We believe she is saving it for a special occasion...

45

As soon as it was printed,
Mia's words began to **spread,**

STARFISH ACADEMY

and the school **buzzed** with **excitement**
at the **front-page** news that said . . .

46

The Mermail

A ROYAL VISIT!

Written by Mermaid Mia

Queen Marina

The Royal Palace

Her Highness, Queen Marina will be visiting our school. She's heard of the academy and wants to meet us all!

It was all the **mermaids** talked about: the **best** news of the year!

In class, they'd whisper **happily**: "The **Queen** is coming HERE!"

I can't wait!

I bet we'll have a ball.

But soon the **news** got out of hand, which made poor **Mia** fret.

And as the day drew closer, she kept **hoping** they'd **forget**.

With one week left, she told her friends:

"I've made a **big mistake.** The **queen's** not **really** visiting – the news I wrote was **fake!**"

"You **should** have told the **truth**," said Fay.
"But now we need a **plan**.
We'll tell the queen what happened
and then **fix** this if we can."

So **Mia** sent a **letter**
to the queen's **royal** address.

Queen Marina
The Royal Palace
Under the Sea

Collections:
Mon-Fri
7am

Please do not
put shells in
the mailbox.

She asked the queen to **help** them out,
and **hoped** that she'd say **yes**.

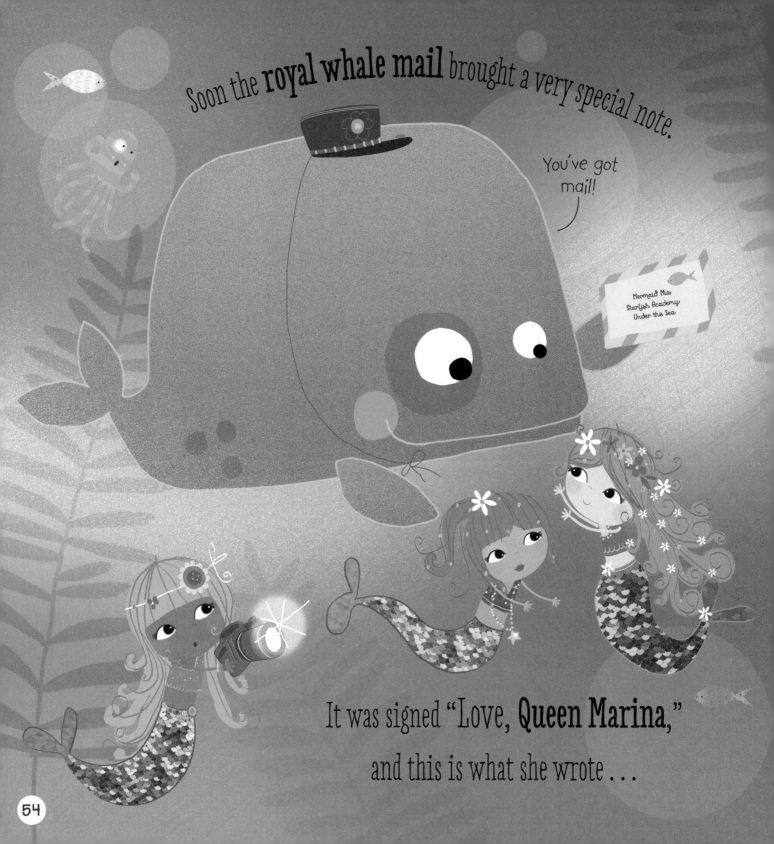

Soon the **royal whale mail** brought a very special note.

You've got mail!

Mermaid Mia
Starfish Academy
Under the Sea

It was signed "Love, **Queen Marina**,"
and this is what she wrote . . .

Dear Mia,

You're very brave for owning up —
it's not easy to do.
And thank you for inviting me,
I'd love to visit you!

Love,
Queen Marina

At last, the **special** day arrived;
the **mermaids** couldn't wait.

YOU'RE GREAT!

They lined the school with **pretty flags**, and a **sign** that said, "YOU'RE GREAT!"

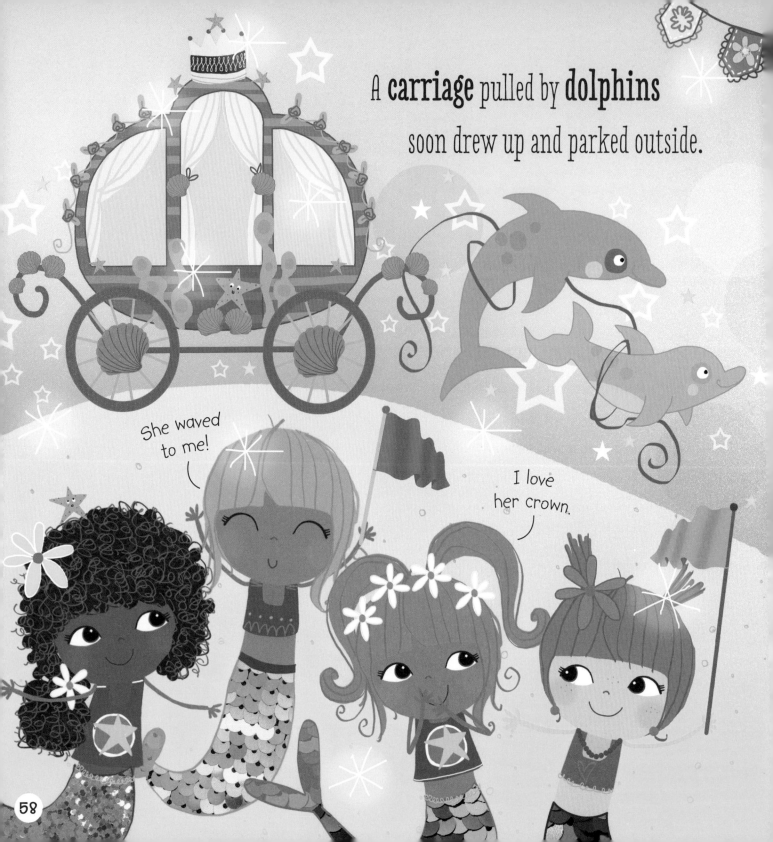

A **carriage** pulled by **dolphins** soon drew up and parked outside.

She waved to me!

I love her crown.

The **queen** swam up to meet them all, and Mia **beamed** with **pride**.

The day was so **amazing**, Mia knew what she **should** do.

Miss Isabella meets Queen Marina

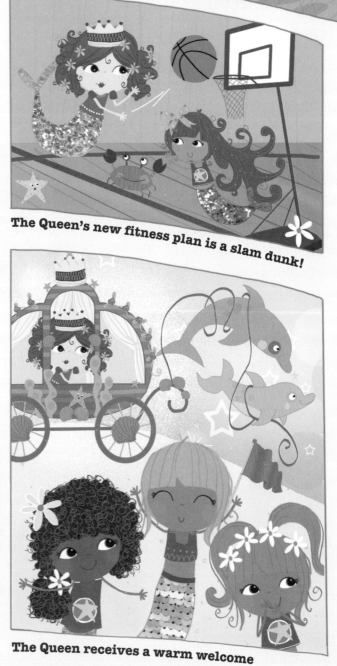

The Queen's new fitness plan is a slam dunk!

The Queen receives a warm welcome

Star student shows off her winning formula

She put the story in the **news**, and every word was **true**.

Everyone had a sea-riously good time!

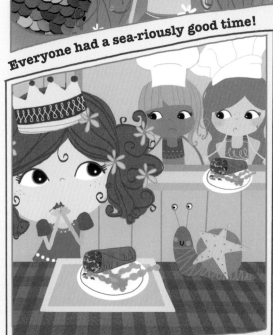

Snail surprise

A ROYAL SUCCESS!

Written by Mermaid Mia

We had a great time yesterday
with Queen Marina here.
And as she left, she told us all:
"I'll come again next year!"

After that, **Mia** was **truthful,**
even when the news was **slow.**

The Mermail

SHELL SHOCK:
Snails spotted
in the canteen!

She'd **learned** that being **honest**
was the **only** way to **go!**

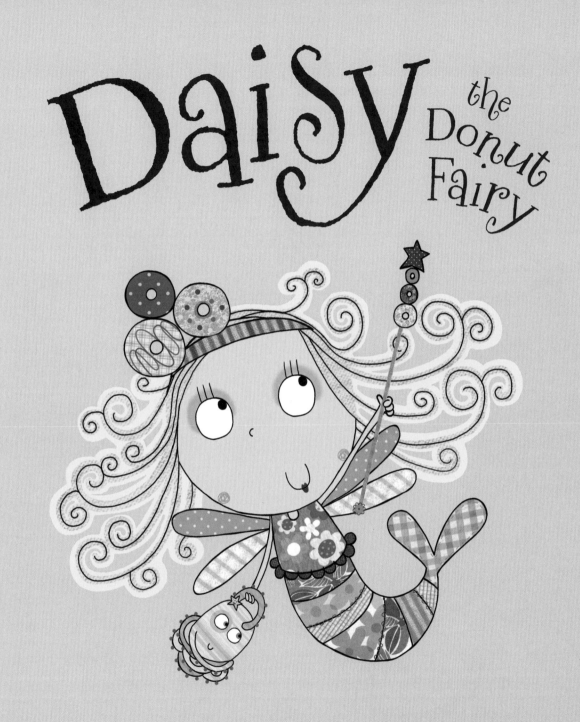

Daisy the Donut Fairy

Tim Bugbird · Lara Ede

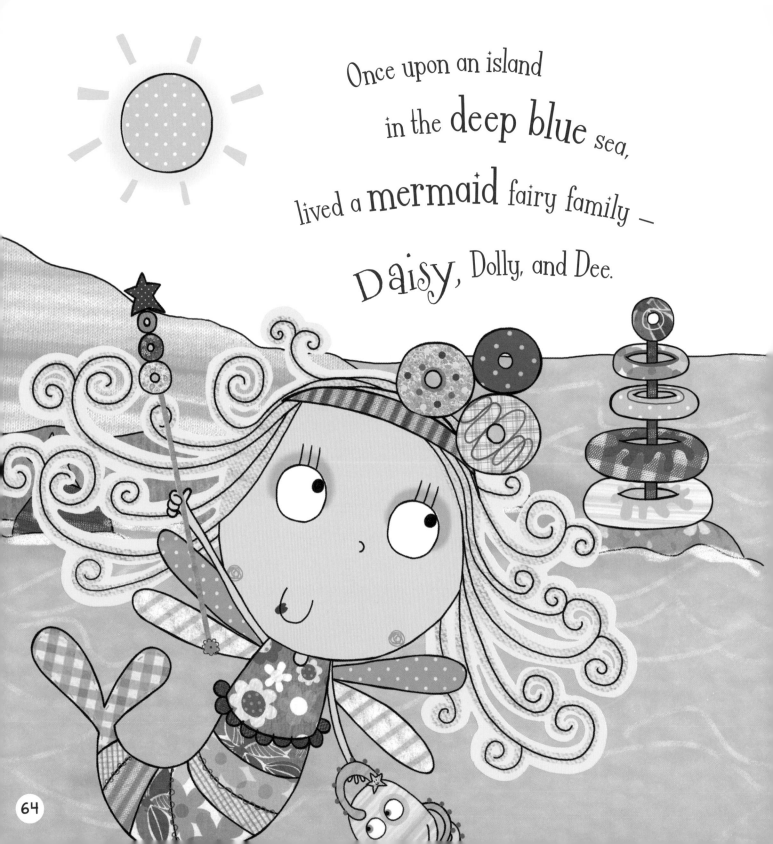

Once upon an island
in the **deep blue** sea,
lived a **mermaid** fairy family —
Daisy, Dolly, and Dee.

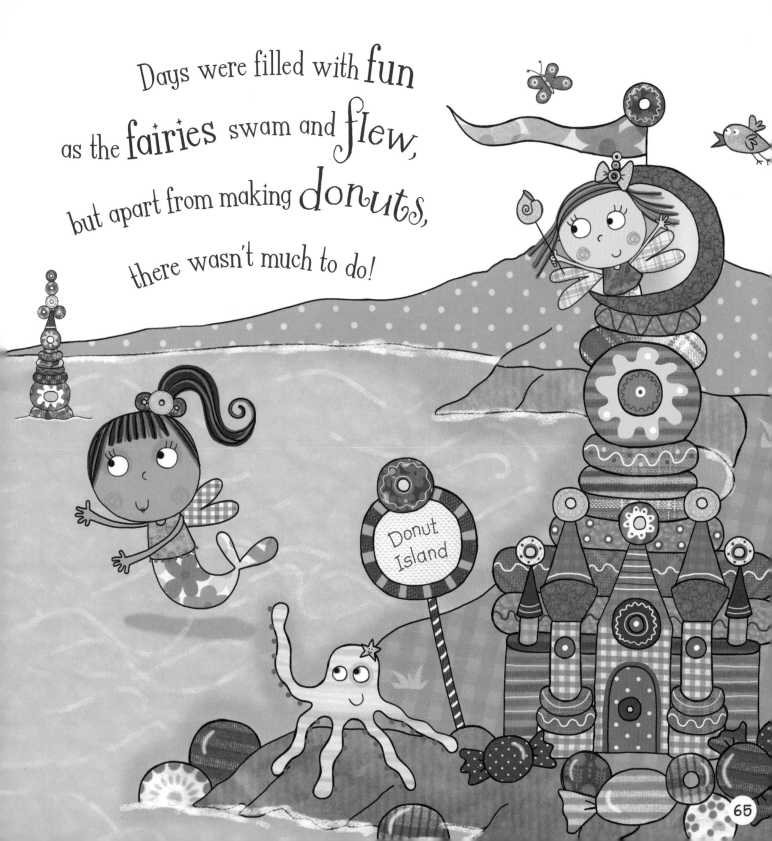

Days were filled with fun
as the fairies swam and flew,
but apart from making donuts,
there wasn't much to do!

Donut Island

Their fairy wands made every kind –
hundreds by the hour!

But the donut mountains grew and grew
'til there was no room in their tower.

So Daisy called a meeting of her fairy clan.
They put their heads together — what they needed was a plan!

Daisy, Dee, and Dolly thought hard for **hours** and **hours**.
Finding **uses** for the **donuts** used up all their fairy powers!

Wheels

The **first** idea was Dolly's —
it didn't work the way she **wished**:
the **wheels** looked
good enough to eat
but soon got very **squished**!

Earrings

This was Dee's **best** idea,
but she didn't think it through –
they were far **too big** to dangle,
and the $frosting$
stuck like glue!

Sunglasses

The **third** idea was Daisy's.
At first it seemed quite good,
but **glasses** made from
donuts just don't
work the way they should!

It was nothing less than awful – there was nothing left to try.

At least that's what the **fairies** thought, until a **pirate ship** sailed by.

Pancake Pete was **all aboard**

with first mate Fearsome Fred,

but neither one could see the **rocks**

with the **pancakes** on their heads!

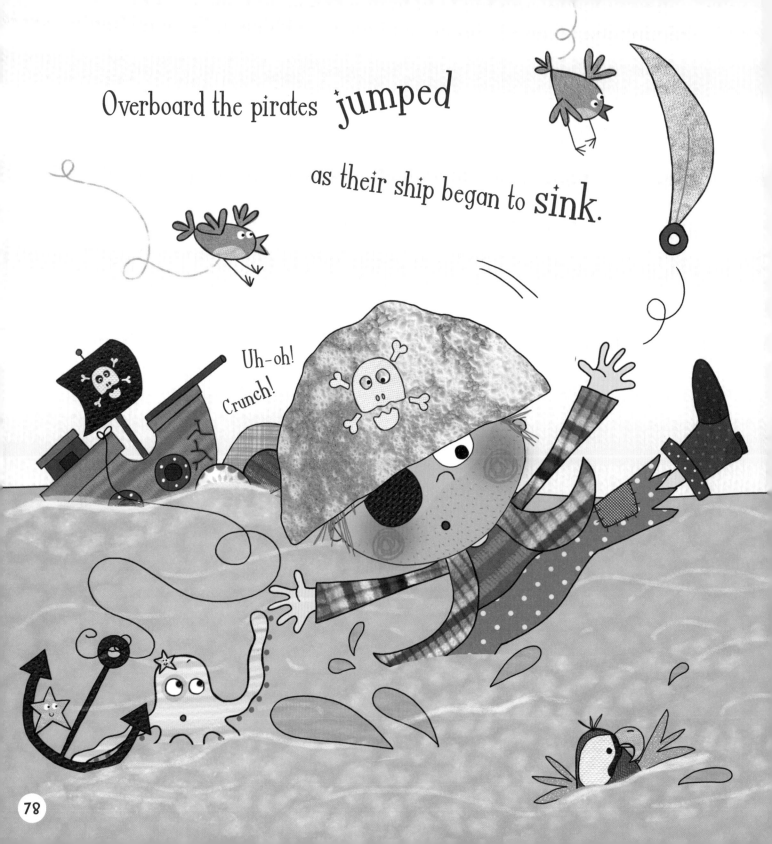

Overboard the pirates jumped
as their ship began to sink.

Uh-oh!
Crunch!

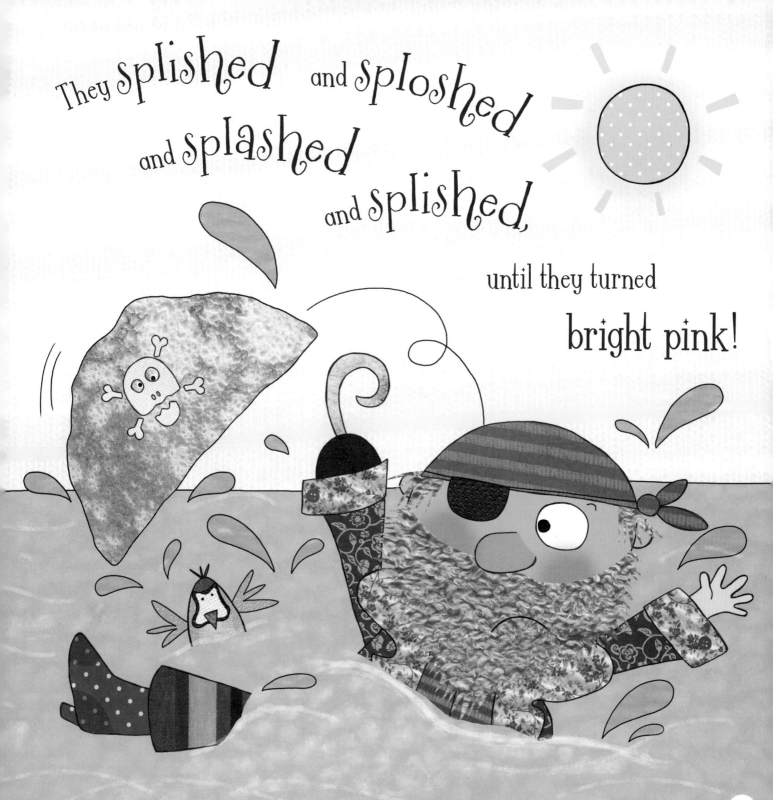

They splished and sploshed and splashed and splished, until they turned bright pink!

Peering through the window
and thinking very **fast**,
Daisy said, "I think we have
a use for these **at last!**"

Donut Island

She took some donuts from the pile and threw them to the boat.

The pirates jumped inside the rings – they really helped them float!

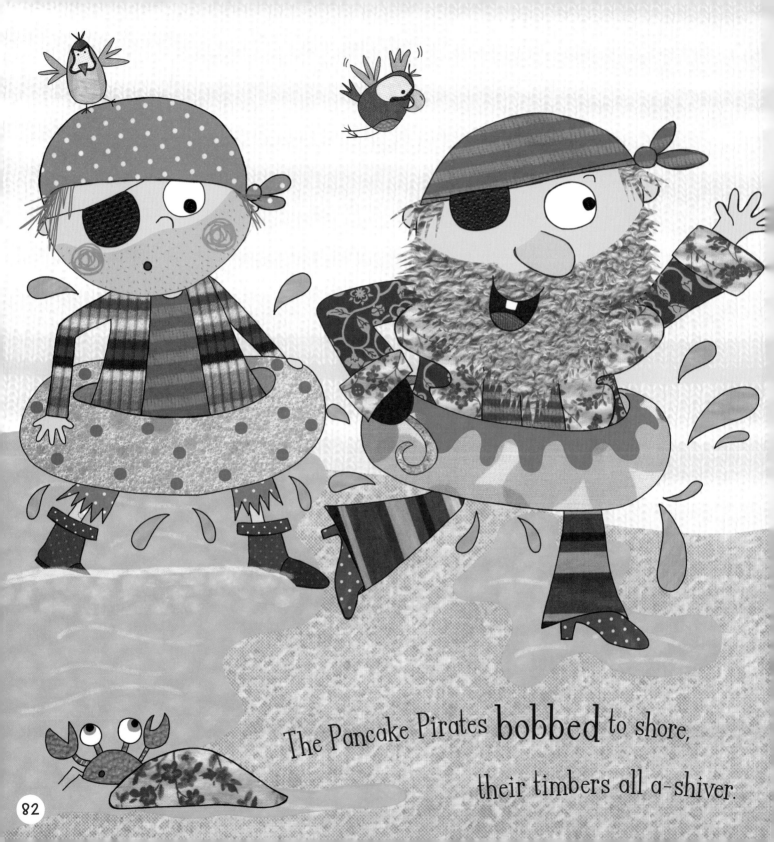

The Pancake Pirates **bobbed** to shore,
their timbers all a-shiver.

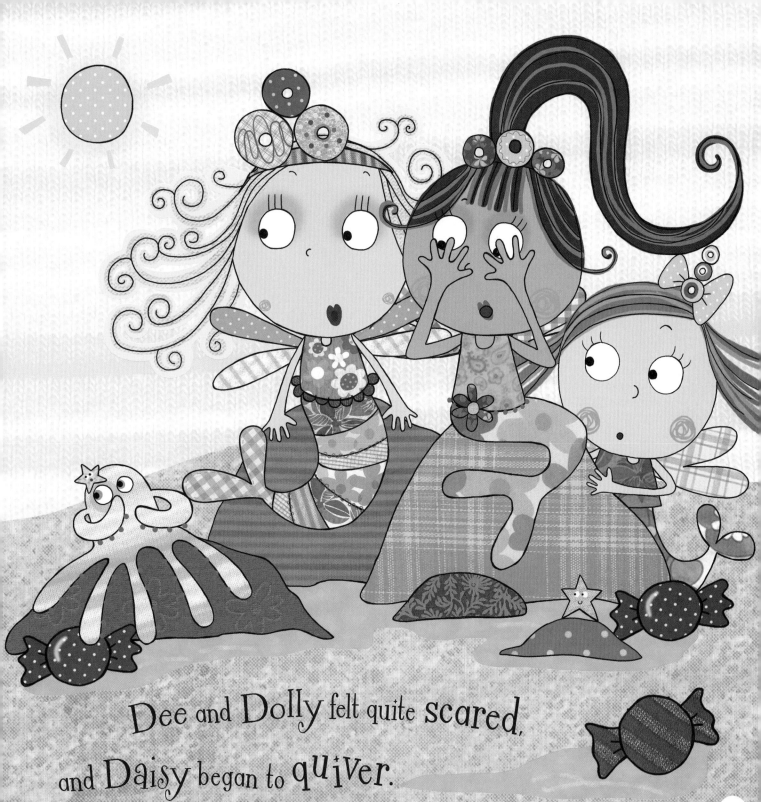

Dee and Dolly felt quite scared,

and Daisy began to quiver.

But Pete said,

"Please don't worry!

We're really not **that** bad,

84

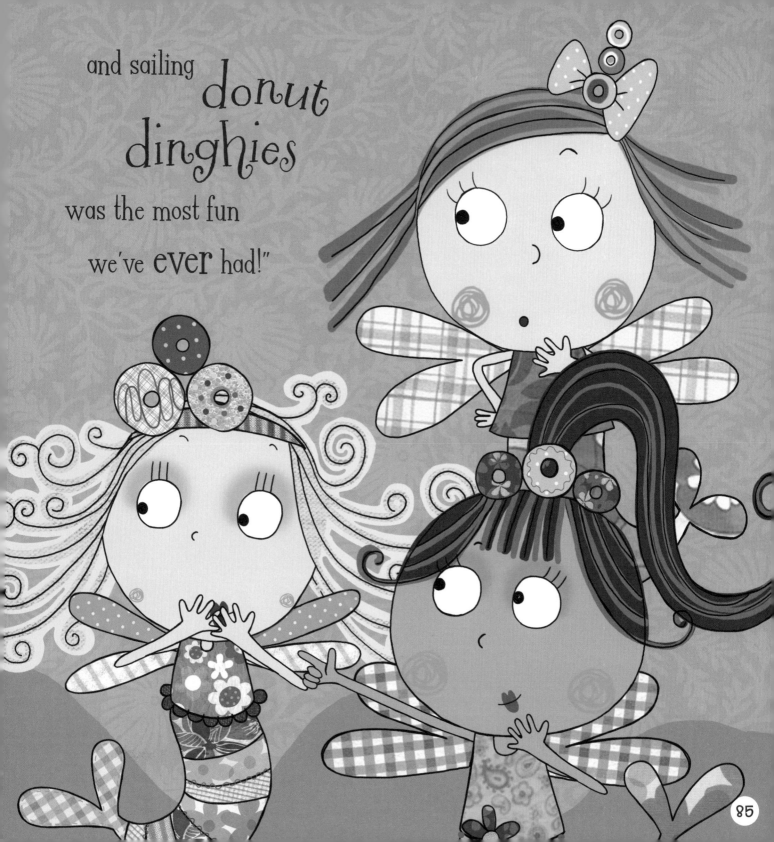

and sailing donut dinghies was the most fun we've ever had!"

85

The Pirates were so grateful, and asked,

"What can we do?"

Daisy said,

"There's a job for us
in sea search and rescue!"

So the fairies and the pirates learned how to work together, helping those in trouble at sea or lost in stormy weather.

Every day was an adventure,
hard work but full of fun,
and their donuts
had a use at last –

every single one!

So that's how Daisy's donuts stopped the pirates from sinking and a mermaid fairy saved the day with true friends and quick thinking!

Meghan Sparkle
and the ROYAL BaBy

Lara Ede · Rosie Greening

Once, in **Coral Kingdom**, an announcement came to say that a brand-new **royal baby** had been born that very day!

The King & Queen have a new baby called Bubble!

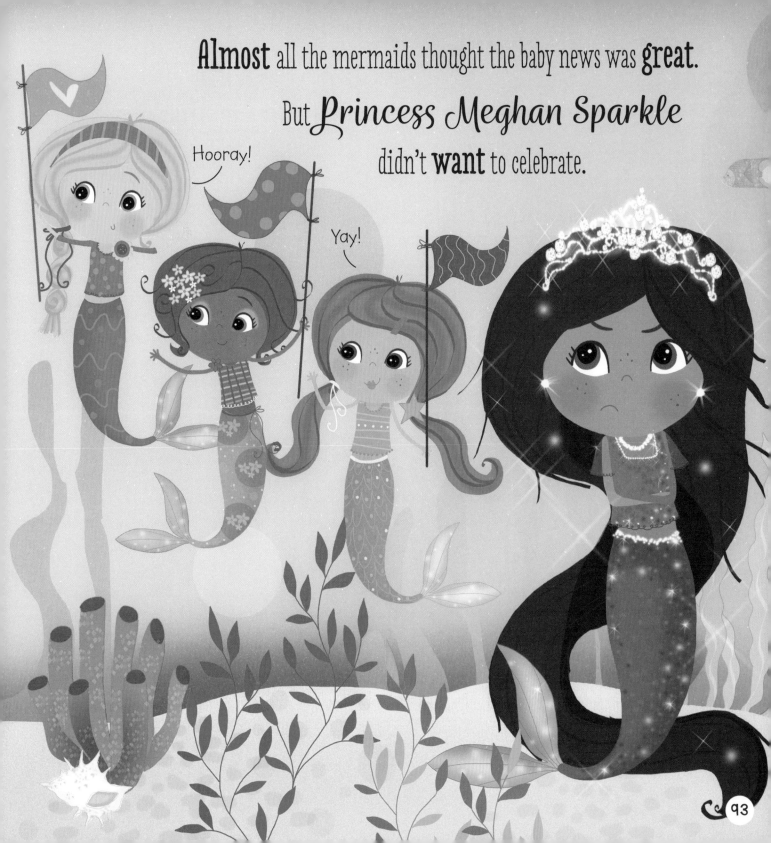

Almost all the mermaids thought the baby news was **great**.
But *Princess Meghan Sparkle* didn't **want** to celebrate.

93

She was baby Bubble's **sister**, but she found it all a **bore**.
From *Meghan's* point of view, her life was going **fine** before!

She could **play games** in the castle or **sing loudly** if she chose...

La - la - LAA!

...and always found a **quiet** place
to **read** a book or **doze**.

But now, the baby **screamed** so much,
it drove her up the wall,
and **smelled** so bad that Meghan
couldn't concentrate at all!

Wahhhh

Wahhhhhhhhh!

One day, **Meghan** couldn't wait to read her book somewhere, when suddenly the sound of Bubble's **crying** filled the air.

but every room was **smelly**...

Wahhhh!

Wahhhh!

Wahhhh!

So **Meghan** searched for somewhere **far away** from all the noise, full...

or **stuffed** with baby toys!

She slammed her book closed with a SMACK and shouted,

"IT'S NOT FAIR!

MER-TALES

Everyone's gone baby mad: I can't read ANYWHERE."

Wahhhhhhhhh!
wahhh!

She sped outside and swam along
a winding path at speed,
until she found a silent spot:
the **PERFECT** place to read!

Meghan read her book for **hours**,
as **happy** as a clam.

But **when** she tried to leave,
she cried...

"I don't know where I am!"

Clownfish Corner

She swam out here so **quickly**,
she'd forgotten to keep track.
And now she simply **didn't know**
which path would take her back!

Just when she felt **lost at sea**,
the princess heard a cough.
The **mail-turtle** was swimming by,
dropping parcels off.

Seaweed Stables

Whale Way

"**Your Royal Highness!**" Turtle cried,
and gave a little bow.

"Can you help me?" **Meghan** asked.
"I've **lost my way** somehow!"

"I'll take you home," said Turtle, "but I **must** drop off this mail."
"That sounds fun!" the mermaid said, and joined him on his trail.

First, he had a parcel for the **clownfish** family,
who all lived **cramped together** in a small anemone.

Thanks, Turtle!

"That looks **crowded**," Meghan thought,
and watched the clownfish play.
"I'm **lucky** I don't share a room
with Bubble every day."

Ooooh!

Ooooooooooh!

A choir **singing** whale songs
was the next stop on their rounds.

But **Meghan** couldn't **understand**
the group's **unusual** sounds.

Oooooooh!

Ooooooooooh!

Turtle laughed:
"That's how they **speak**;
it just sounds odd to **you**."

Meghan thought of **Bubble's cries**...
could they mean something too?

They went to **Seaweed Stables** for their last delivery.
The little baby seahorses were racing with a

"wheeeeeee!"

This is fun!

I was born to win!

Meghan and the turtle
watched the babies for a while.

"Maybe siblings **are** ok,"
thought Meghan with a smile.

With the packages delivered,
Meghan thought of what she'd seen.
And **suddenly** she realized
how **silly** she had been!

She said, "I **understand** now
that when all is said and done,
having someone **new** around
is going to be **fun!**"

The turtle guided **Meghan** back across the ocean floor,
and soon she heard a distant cry she **knew** she'd heard before.

Wahhhhhhh!

"Thank you, Turtle!"
Meghan said.
"I recognize those sounds."
And then she followed Bubble's cries
into the castle grounds.

She rushed to **hug** the baby, feeling happy as can be.
"Hello Bubble," *Meghan* said. "I'm glad we're family."

After that, she didn't leave the royal baby's side, and read her **favorite** books aloud whenever Bubble cried.

So Meghan found some lovely friends, and as young Bubble grew,

she saw that life is wonderful when you are one of two!

Lola the Lollipop Fairy

Tim Bugbird · Lara Ede

Once upon a time
in a circus big top,
lived a fairy family,
the sisters Lollipop!

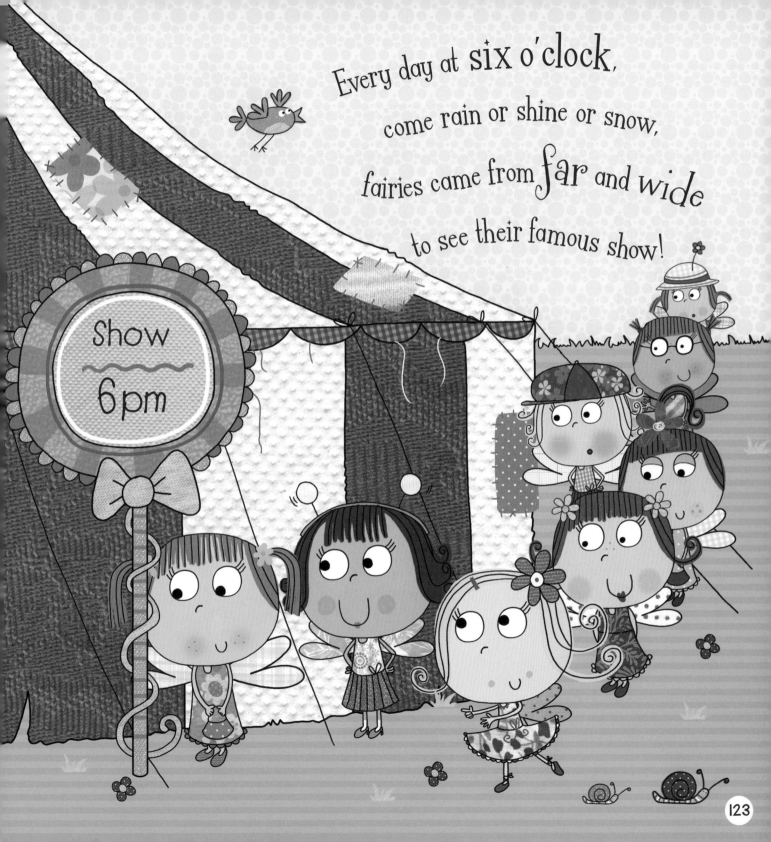

Every day at six o'clock,
come rain or shine or snow,
fairies came from far and wide
to see their famous show!

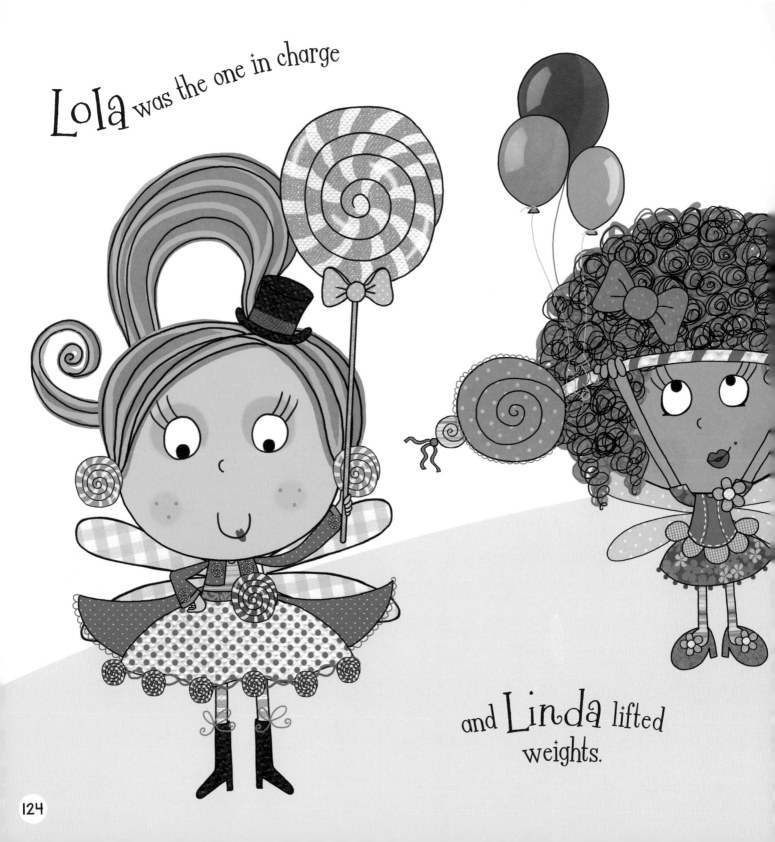

Lola was the one in charge

and Linda lifted weights.

124

Lulu juggled lollipops
and sometimes spinning plates!

Their act had been the same for years
and their tent was worn and old,
but every night they did their best
and all the seats were sold.

'Til one morning Lola woke;
she **yawned** and rubbed her eyes.
She looked outside and had a **shock** –
what a bad surprise!

Next door, where the grass had been,

the plants and trees and flowers,

there stood a brand-new **theme park**

with **rides** and **slides** and **towers!**

cat bed

The park became
the **place to go**,
where fairies met to play,
and **no one**
came to Lola's show.

She sighed, as if to say,
"The rides are so exciting,
we just cannot **compete**."

Lulu said, "Let's face it, friends,
I think we might be **beat!**"

helter-skelter

"So we'll just make our show **better!**"
Lola boldly cried.
"We'll do our **best**, so if we fail,
at least we'll know we tried!"

"Let's think of something **super big**,
a **spectacular** creation,
a show to make the fairies talk —
we'll be the new **sensation!**"

In a flash it came to Lola —
a plan to make them swoon.

Lola the Fairy Cannonball

would fly up to the moon!

So the fairies built a **cannon**
that was just the perfect size
to fire fearless Lola
from the circus to the skies!
They **banged** and **bashed**,
and **clanged** and **clashed**
until the job was done.
The work was **hard**,
the hours were **long**,
but they'd never had **such fun!**

PLAN

FAIRY TOOLS

The day for launching Lola
came around really fast.
Linda hollered, "Three, two, one!"
and, with a deafening BLAST,

Lola shot up into space
as the fairies waved and cheered.
And Lola thought, "What a lovely place,
I'm glad I volunteered!"

And when Lola finally landed, she cried:

"Oh my goodness, golly!
I thought the moon was made of cheese,
but it's a great big orange lolly!"

It certainly was the sweetest place
Lola had **ever seen,**
with **lollipops** of every kind
and mountains of whipped **cream!**

The **air** was
sweet as **strawberries**
and the **sky** was
pink and **clear**.
Lola flew back down to earth –
she'd had a **new idea**.

Her cannon show had been a blast,

but this plan was the ace.

They'd make their fairy fortunes

firing fairies into space!

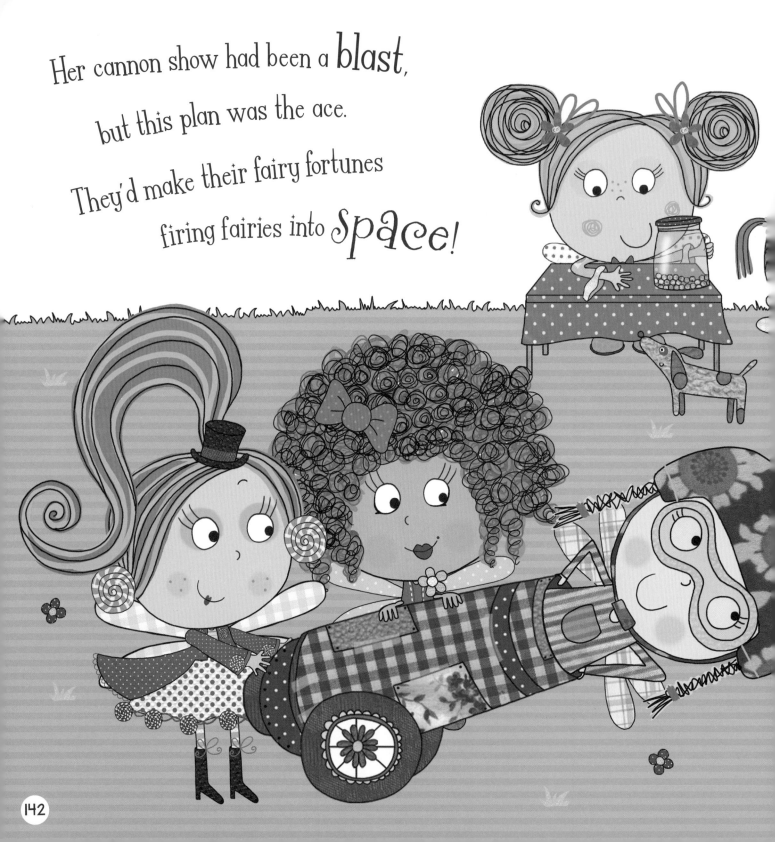

And so the sisters got to work, they never seemed to stop.
Soon the moon trips made enough to buy a

new BIG TOP!

With a brand-new sparkly cannon, glitter, and lights aglow,
very soon the stage was set for their amazing circus show!

It was thrilling and exciting, a full house every night.
The fairies saved the circus thanks to Lola's daring flight!

145

So Lola, Linda, and Lulu made the **perfect** team.

By working hard, and not giving up, they lived their **fairy dream!**

Just NARWHAL

Lara Ede • Rosie Greening

Narwhal was a whale who thought she had **no skills** at all.

She couldn't **cook** . . .

Recipe

or **knit** . . .

or **sing** . . .

or even
catch a ball!

Meanwhile, all her **mermaid** friends were skillful as can be.
If they tried out something **new**, they did it **perfectly**.

"Wow!" thought Narwhal every day.
"There's nothing they can't do.
But I'm **just Narwhal,**
and I wish that I had **talent** too."

One morning, Star and Coral
cried to **Narwhal** in distress:

"Our **art contest** has started,
but everything's a **mess!**"

STAR

MARINA

"We need a **judge**," said Coral,
"and our time is nearly up.
Can **you** judge our paintings
and decide who wins this **cup?**"

SANDY

ISLA

CORAL

Narwhal thought,
"I'll get it wrong,"
and quickly shook her head.
She told them, "I'm just Narwhal -
I'll find someone else instead."

155

She asked **Cackle the Clownfish**
to decide which art should win.

ISLA

"The prize goes to the

FUNNIEST!"

said Cackle with a grin.

Haha!

Haha!

Narwhal thought,
"That's not enough to win the special prize.
But I'm **just Narwhal**, so I'll check
with someone **big** and **wise**."

157

She found a **big blue whale** and asked,
"Which painting is the **best?**"

"The
BIGGEST!"
shouted Jumbo.
"**Forget** about the rest!"

"I'm not sure size is **everything**," said Narwhal quietly.
"But since I am **just Narwhal**,
I'll make sure **Shelly** agrees."

Shelly scuttled around the art, but judged them **selfishly**.
The shellfish said, "The **winner** is the one that features . . .

ME!"

MARINA

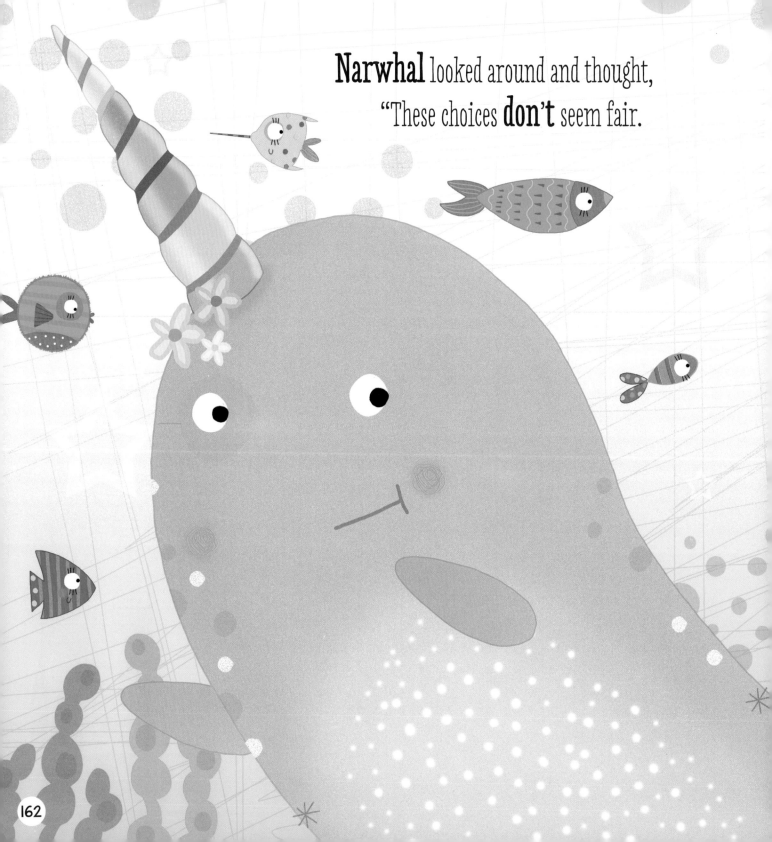

Narwhal looked around and thought,
"These choices **don't** seem fair.

ISLA

CORAL

MARINA

They **can't** judge on **one thing** alone:
there's **much** more to compare."

Narwhal swam to join her friends.
"I've let you down!" she cried.

"You need a **fair** and **honest** judge,
who sees how **hard** you tried."

The mermaids said, "If that's the case,
then **YOU** should judge our art!
To us, you're not '**just Narwhal**,'
and we'd **love** you to take part."

Narwhal gave a nervous smile and said, "Okay, I'll try!"

STAR

MARINA

ISLA

And she wrote a list of **qualities** to judge the paintings by.

Narwhal swam around the art,
and **studied** each with care.
She looked at **every** brush stroke
to make sure that she was **fair**.

- Colors ☑
- Theme ☑
- Brushstroke ☐
- Technique ☐
- Effort ☐
- Beauty ☐

SANDY

At last she said, "Each piece of art
is **special** in its way.
But **ONE** checked every box for me . . .

Star wins first prize today!"

1ST

STAR

Star held up the shining cup
for **everyone** to see.
Then Coral rushed to Narwhal,
and she **hugged** her gratefully.

She said, "You are the **finest** judge
we could have ever found.
You're **fair** and **open-minded**...

the most **just** narwhal around!"

From that day on, **Narwhal** would judge **each** contest she could find.

FINISH

And though she couldn't dance or sing, at last, she didn't **mind**.

She thought,

"My **skills** are hidden –
they're not **obvious** to see.
But just like all the **paintings,**

there is so much
more to me!"

Sparkle Town Fairies

Daphne
the
Diamond
Fairy

Sarah Creese * Lara Ede

On **Sparkle Town's** main shopping street,
there stood a grand **boutique**,

filled with **dresses**, hats, and shoes
so cute, and oh-so-chic!

DIAMOND BOUTIQUE

Every **dress** was quite unique —
but one thing did not vary:
each stitch and style was made by hand
by **Daphne** the **Diamond Fairy**.

Diamonds
are always
in style.

The fairies flocked from miles around
to buy each new design –
at times poor Daphne had to shout,
"Please, darlings, wait in line!"

Ooh,
I love it!

MADE BY DAPHNE

MADE BY DAPHNE

MADE BY DAPHNE

MADE BY DAPHNE

First she sketched

and next she cut,

then it was time
to **sew**

in every color imaginable.
And lastly, for **extra glow**...

she swished her special **sparkle wand**,
and with a twinkling smile

Perfect!

there appeared a **dazzling diamond** –
her signature fairy style.

181

One morning Daphne left for work,
but as she turned the corner,

High Street

a letter carried by **Fluttermail**
unfurled itself before her.

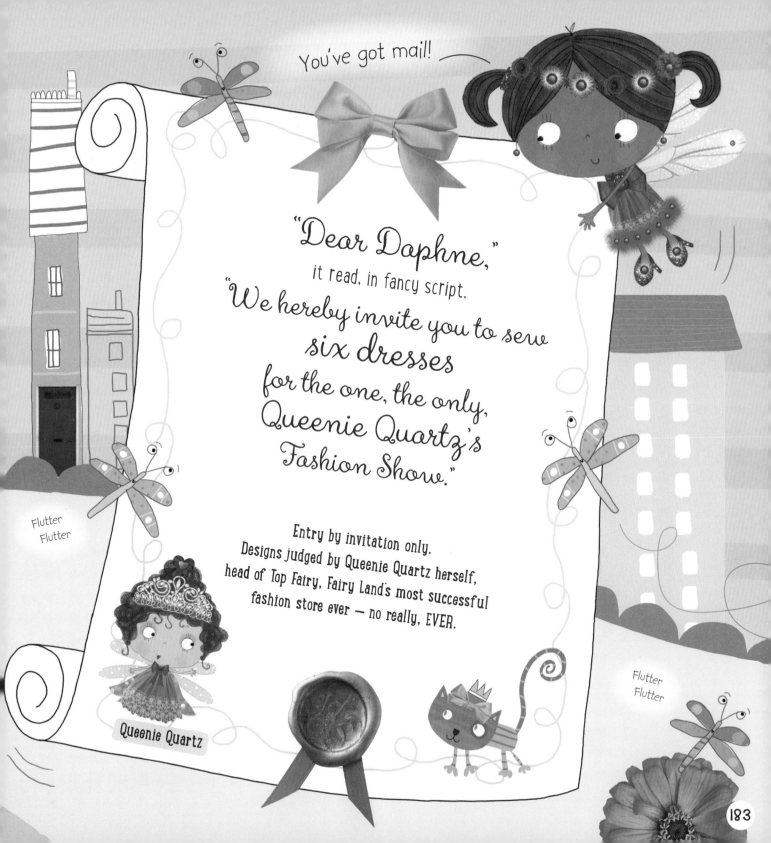

You've got mail!

"Dear Daphne,"
it read, in fancy script.
"We hereby invite you to sew
six dresses
for the one, the only,
Queenie Quartz's
Fashion Show."

Entry by invitation only.
Designs judged by Queenie Quartz herself,
head of Top Fairy, Fairy Land's most successful
fashion store ever — no really, EVER.

Flutter
Flutter

Queenie Quartz

Flutter
Flutter

Filled with glee,
she **whizzed** to work
to start her dress collection.

"It has to be my best," she said.
"To win I need perfection."

All day and night
she **waved** her wand
but nothing seemed
quite right.

Swish!
Swoosh!

Then by chance
she tripped
and swished!

Swoo-oops!

From her wand
came a **wondrous sight...**

A shower of **glittering diamonds**,
covering each and every dress.

Daphne blinked from the diamonds' dazzle.
This look was **THE ONE** to impress!

The next day, Daphne's friends arrived
to be fitted for the show.
Daphne revealed her new designs
and they **gasped** at the glamorous glow.

You look
dazzling.

No, you look
dazzling.

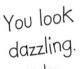

But seeing her friends look so sublime,
Daphne's thoughts turned jealous and sour.
"Why should **they** be the ones to shine
and steal my finest hour?"

Daphne, these are sparkletastic!

Hmm.

And in a whirl
she frowned,
then **snapped**,
"I'm afraid this
just won't do.
My **creations**
are far too good —
they'll look
better on **ME**
than you."

I'll wear ALL of them.

Soon, the **show day** came around,
and Daphne was well-prepared.

Her friends, meanwhile, sat at the back
(they were hurt, but they still cared).

Backstage, fairies flitted about
so no one saw Queenie's cat,

who chased a feathery bird
(well, a dress)
causing a **catastrophe** that...

knocked a pole,

Clunk

made a rug unroll.

Slip

Slide

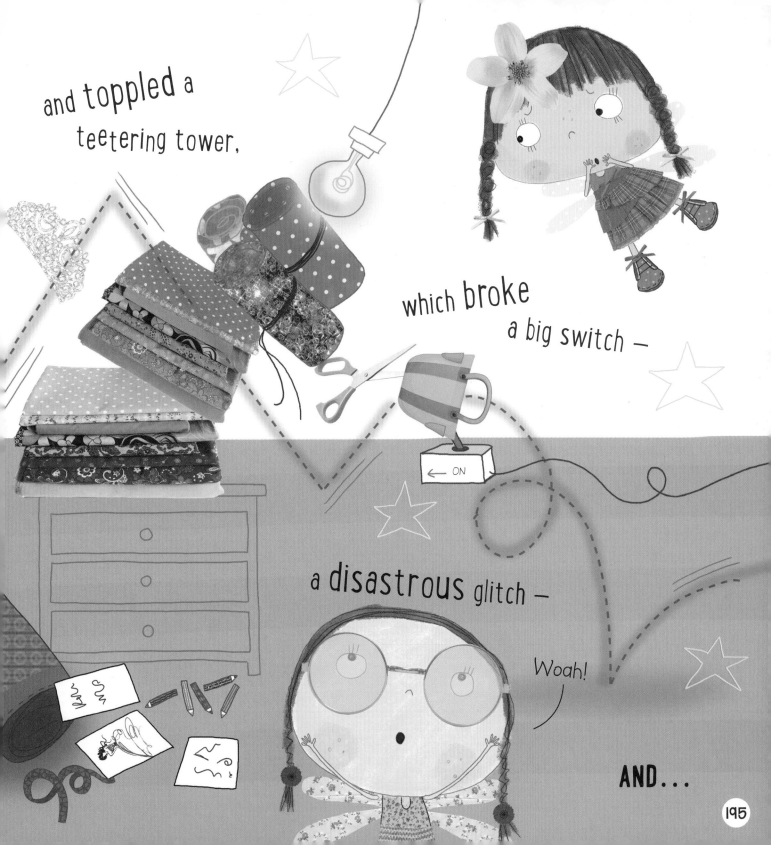

and toppled a teetering tower,

which broke a big switch —

a disastrous glitch —

Woah!

AND...

195

TURNED OFF ALL THE POWER!

In the dark, the fairies flapped,
but Daphne had an **idea**.
By wand-light, something caught her eye
and made the **answer** clear.

"I can't do this alone," she thought,
and **rushed** to find her friends.
"I know now I was wrong," she said.
"Can we ever make amends?
I'm **sorry** for being selfish;
it was mean and unfair, too."
The fairies **smiled**, then **hugged** their friend
and said, "What can we do?"

Here's
the plan...

She gave each friend a **diamond dress**, then told them where to go.
"Fairies at the ready," she cried, "it's time to save this **show!**"

Who needs lights!

Daphne swooshed her diamond wand — up high, then left to right.
She bounced a beam from dress to dress, filling the room with **LIGHT!**

The show was such a great success
that Queenie had to say,

"Dear Daphne, will you come each year
to be our **light display?**"

203

And though the fairies' dresses
sparkled beyond compare,
the thing that **sparkled** most of all
was the **friendship** that they **shared!**

Groovicorns in the city

Rosie Greening • Stuart Lynch

In far-off Funky Forest
lived a friendly **dancing** crew
who were WAY more cool than unicorns
(and much politer, too!)

Psst . . .
sometimes
I'm cool!

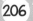

This group was called the

GROOVICORNS,

and when you saw their moves,

you couldn't help but join the fun

and get into the groove!

One sunny day, an **acorn** note came for the **dancing troop**, from a **squirrel** in the **city** who knew the **groovy** group.

Squirrel's Treehouse
Central Park
Moanhattan

Dear groovicorns,

Moanhattan needs your dancing: everyone is GLUM. Please come to the city and help them all have fun!

Love Squirrel xxx

"Let's do it!" cried the groovicorns.

"The city's not that far.

We'll cheer them up, and then come back for Prancing With The Stars!"

LET'S DANCE!

TV GUIDE

They **left** their Funky Forest friends
and jumped on board a **ferry**.
They were off to **help out** Squirrel
and to make Moanhattan **merry**!

S.S. Groove

Moanhattan City

Beep! Beep! Beep! Beep!

But when they reached the **city**, it was much **worse** than they'd feared.

"Where's the **sunshine?**"

"What's that **smell?**"

"It's really **gray** and **weird!**"

Cafe **GLOOM!**

WALK

WIFI!

LET'S DANCE!

The worst bit was the **gloomycorns** who acted like **machines**.

They never **smiled** . . .

or said **hello** . . .

. . . they just **stared** at their **screens!**

They found a square with glaring screens
all going flicker–flash.

WIFI!

MORE
DATA

MANE SQUARE

MOVIES

They took a breath,
cried, "6, 7, 8 . . ."
and then began to . . .

215

CRASH!!!

Watch it!

Look out!

Eek!

Ouch!

The gloomycorns bumped into them, distracted by their phones. "They won't look up!" cried Ziggy, with a big, un-groovy groan.

216

They went down to the **subway**, where the gloomycorns looked **bored**.
But with all the **screens** and **headphones**, every dance move was **ignored!**

They breakdanced,

flossed,

and did the **dab**,

but no **routine** would do.

The **gloomycorns** were in the **cloud**,
and **nothing** could get through.

"This is hopeless!" cried the group.
"Those screens are all they see."

Do-nut
(smile)

So they sadly trotted off
to visit Squirrel in her tree.

Moanhattan
Park

219

Squirrel said, "Don't worry, guys –
you tried your **best**, I know.
Could you **teach me** some dance moves
before you have to go?"

So the groovicorns explained their steps, and Squirrel had such fun, that she filmed them on her acorn phone . . .

Step left...turn around...
hands in the air...
step right...star jump!

...to **watch** once they were done.

When they watched the video,
it filled them all with cheer.
It was happy, fun, and colorful
and gave them an idea . . .

They posted it on HoofTube
and as quickly as can be,

it appeared on every screen
for all the gloomycorns to see!

223

All across the city, everybody learned the moves, and the gloomycorns put down their phones to get into the groove.

224

There was **SINGING** in the subways . . .

. . . and **SWIRLING** in the street.

The gloomycorns were having **fun** and **dancing** to the beat!

225

After that, Moanhattan shone with laughter, life, and color, as the gloomycorns all learned to laugh and talk to one another.

And **back at home**, the groovicorns were keeping **busy** too.

They were **filming** groovy **dances** . . .

227

...for EVERYONE to do!

Molly the Muffin Fairy

Tim Bugbird · Lara Ede

Molly the Muffin Fairy was famous in Fairyland for making perfect muffins — some small and some quite grand.

Each one was baked 'til **spongy,**
golden, soft, and sweet.
Her wand put in big **blueberries**
to make the **treats** complete!

Blueberries

Blueberries

The **blueberries** came in boxes, delivered by Mel and Kerri,

her two **best friends**, who drove a truck
shaped like a **giant berry!**

233

But then one day when **baking**,
Molly's temper began to **fray**;

her **muffins** had no softness —
she was having a **bad** bake day!

Her baking got **no better**,
and soon **Molly's** fairy home
was full of **rubbery muffins**
with tops as hard as **stone!**

237

Molly was not happy. The baking was making her MAD!

She fussed and fumed and finally flipped!

What she did was really bad . . .

She grabbed a tray of muffins and threw them to the floor,
then took a muffin in her hand and hurled it out the door!

The muffin hit her trampoline and **bounced** up in the air.

The strangest scene there's **ever** been followed on from there . . .

241

and pinged
and ponged,

It bounced
and bumped

startling a **squirrel,**
who scampered and woke
a **porcupine** down below!

flying
to and **fro,**

243

Up with a **start**, the porcupine **ran**
to find a **safe place** to hide.

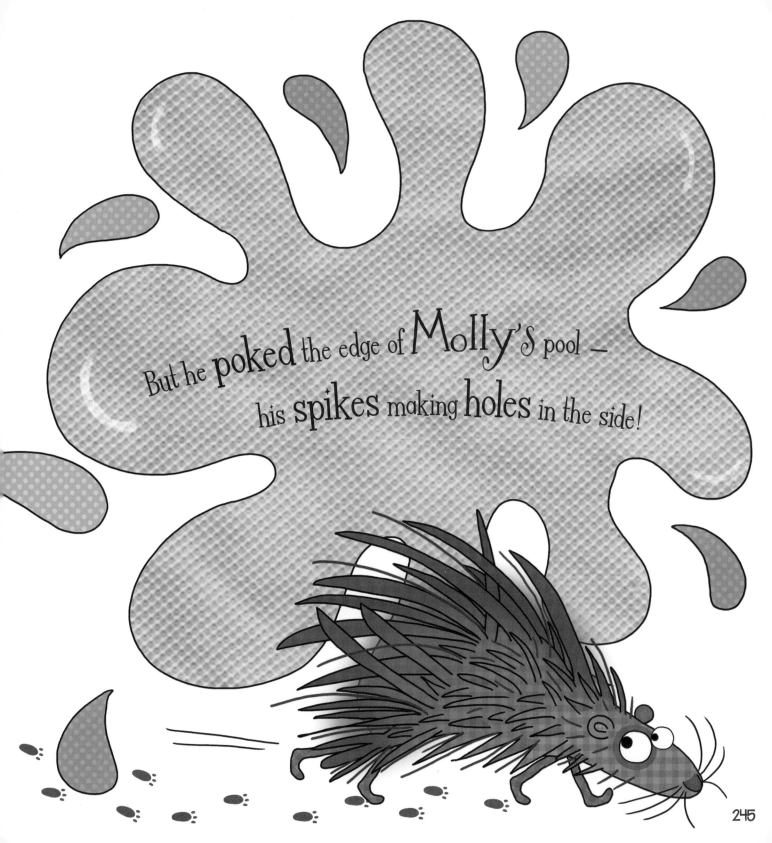

But he **poked** the edge of Molly's pool –
his **spikes** making **holes** in the side!

245

Water gushed out from the holes,

flooding the road all around.

Then Mel and Kerri's truck arrived,
but **how** would they cross the **wet** ground?

Berry Truck

Blueberries

Blueberries

Molly cried, "It's all a mess!"
Mel said, "Oh, stop whining!
Those muffins of yours could help us _
every cloud has a silver lining!"

"Maybe they could make a **path**. Just try and see."

So Molly laid the **muffins** down . . .

and the truck

crossed **easily!**

Berry
Truck

Blueberries

Blueberries

Then, before the **fairies'** eyes,
the **muffins** began to expand.

Soaking up water, they became

the **biggest** in Fairyland!

"The muffins feel soft!" cried Molly.

"Don't eat them, though; they're not clean!

But squashed together, I think they'll make . . ."

"the best-ever trampoline!"

Molly learned that when things look bad, you can always find a way to see things from the **sunny side** and turn around your day!